E
DOO

Dooley, Virginia

I need glasses

DEMCO

I NEED GLASSES

My Visit to the Optometrist

by VIRGINIA DOOLEY

Illustrated by STEPHANIE ROTH

For Lauren, Katie, Devan, Jordan, Mickey, and Michael–V.D.

For Pennie Oakes, surf sister and friend–S.R.

ACKNOWLEDGMENTS
Thanks to Karl Adler, Jr., O.D., Wise Vision Center, and
Karen R. Kudija, O.D.

For information contact:
MONDO Publishing
980 Avenue of the Americas
New York, NY 10018

Visit our web site at http://www.mondopub.com

Printed in the United States of America

02 03 04 05 06 07   9 8 7 6 5 4 3 2 1

ISBN 1-59034-040-X
Designed by Symon Chow

Library of Congress Cataloging-in-Publication Data

Dooley, Virginia, 1956-
     I need glasses : my visit to the optometrist / by Virginia Dooley ; illustrated by
Stephanie Roth.
        p.cm.
     Summary: Nick describes what happened when he went to the optometrist to get glasses.
     ISBN 1-59034-040-X (pbk. : alk. paper)
     [1. Eyeglasses--Fiction. 2. Optometrists--Fiction.] I. Roth, Stephanie, ill. II. Title.

PZ7.D72655 In 2002
[E]--dc21
                                                            2002067785

Good morning, class!

Hi, my name is Nick. I just got glasses.
Here's what happened.

3

One day in school, the nurse gave everyone in my class an eye test.

4

When it was my turn, I covered my left
eye and looked at the chart. Then I covered
my right eye. The chart was blurry.

"You might need glasses," said the nurse.

"Take this note home to your parents."

6

Maybe the nurse was right. Sometimes it was hard to see the chalkboard.

I also had to sit really close to the TV to watch my favorite show.

An optometrist (op-TOM-ih-trist) is a doctor who can test your eyes to find out how well you can see.

My mom made an appointment with an optometrist.

On Saturday, my mom and I went to see the optometrist.

9

The first thing I saw were rows and rows of
eyeglasses. Then, I saw a man in a white coat.
It was Dr. Fox, the eye doctor.

Dr. Fox led us into a room filled with machines I'd never seen before. I was glad my mom was with me.

First, Dr. Fox asked my mom about how often I got sick. Then he asked me if I had any problems seeing.

"Sometimes at school and when I watch TV," I said.

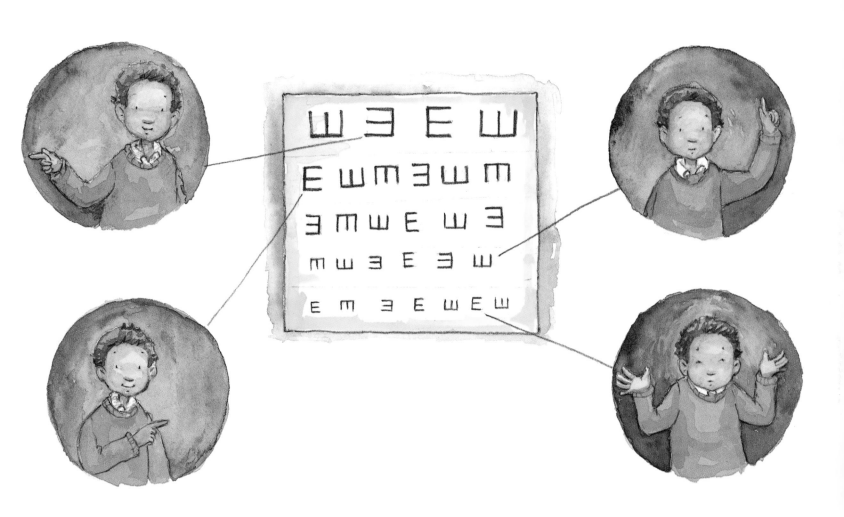

"Okay," said Dr. Fox, "I want you to look at an eye chart."

Dr. Fox turned off the lights. He told me to look at the chart
and point in the direction that the E's on the chart were facing.

13

"Now I'm going to use this machine to look inside your eyes," said Dr. Fox. "The machine won't touch your eyes, and it won't hurt at all."

He was right!

With an autorefractor (AW-toh-re-FRAK-ter), the doctor can find out how well your eyes focus on and see what you are looking at.

14

Then Dr. Fox told me to hold my head very still and follow his finger with my eyes. He needed to make sure my eyes moved the way they should.

Wow, was that hard! I kept wanting to turn my head.

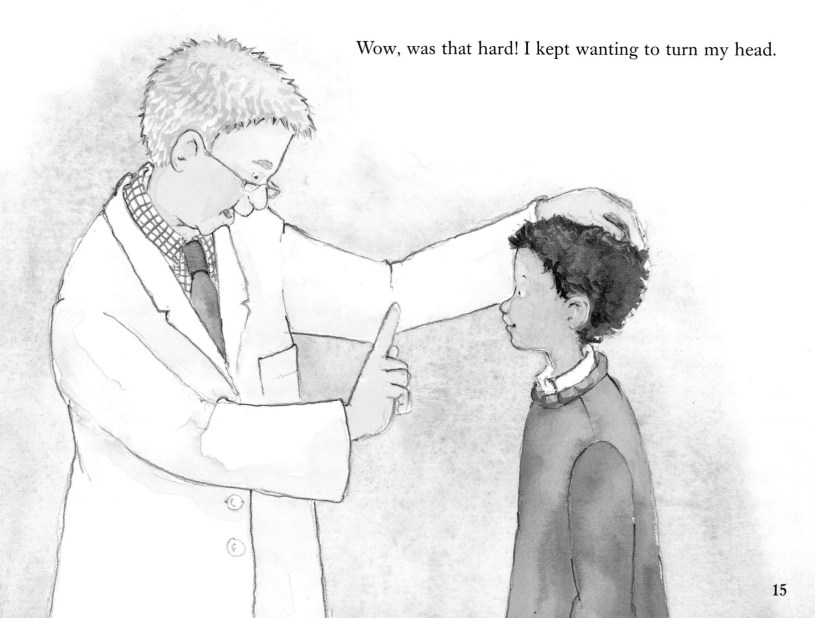

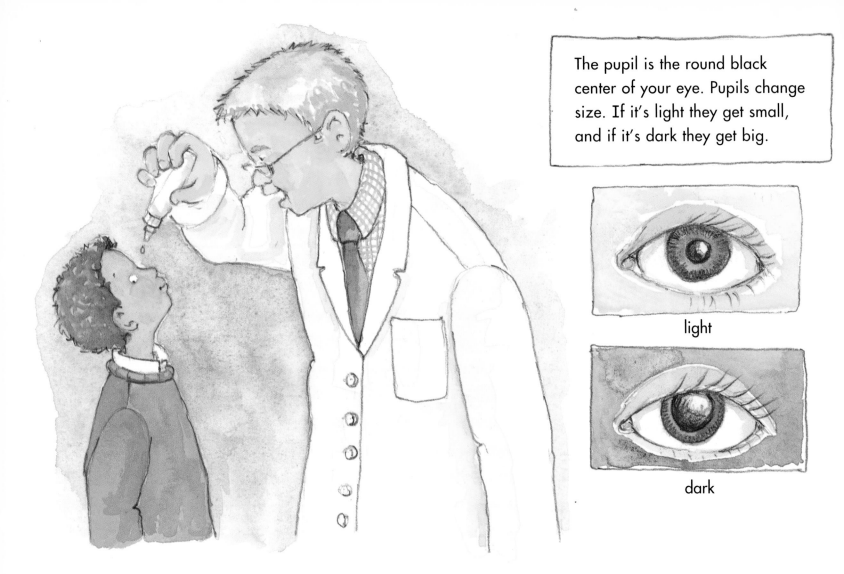

The pupil is the round black center of your eye. Pupils change size. If it's light they get small, and if it's dark they get big.

light

dark

"We're almost done," said Dr. Fox. "Next I'm going to check your pupils with another machine. But first I need to put drops in your eyes."

He put some drops in my eyes. They made everything look blurry.

With a phoropter (foh-ROP-ter), the doctor can put different lenses in front of your eyes and find the lenses that help you see best.

"The drops freeze the muscles in your eyes for a few minutes," said Dr. Fox. "It helps me use this machine to find out when you can see best."

I sat down in front of the other machine.

"Look through here," said Dr. Fox. "I want you to tell me when you can see clearly."

nearsighted

farsighted

Nearsighted people have trouble seeing things far away. Some people are farsighted. They have trouble seeing things that are up close.

"Well, Nick," said Dr. Fox, "all these tests helped me to find out that you're nearsighted. Glasses will help you see much better."

An optician (op-TISH-un) is someone who makes or sells glasses.

Then it was time to pick out the kind of glasses I wanted.

An optician helped me.

19

Some frames were too big.   Some were too small.

Some were just not me.

At last, I found a pair that was just right.

The optician made sure the glasses fit. She also fixed them
so they wouldn't hurt my nose or my ears.

I was worried the first time I wore my glasses to school. What would my friends say about them?

23

Guess what? Everyone liked my new glasses.

Best of all, now I can see much better!